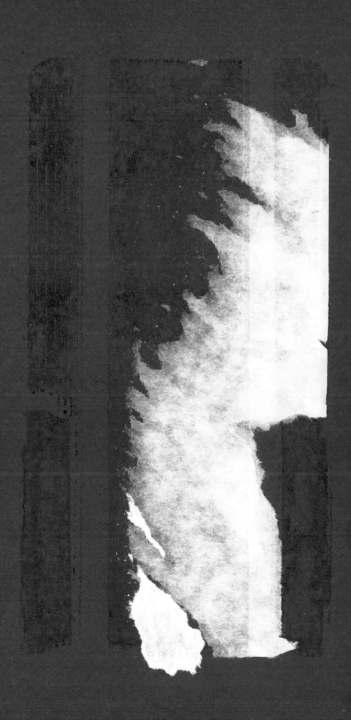

BUZZY WIDGET

BY KEVIN KISER
ILLUSTRATED BY JOHN O'BRIEN

MARSHALL CAVENDISH   NEW YORK

To SuAnn, my Miss Jane
—K.K.

For Tess
—J.O'B.

Marshall Cavendish
99 White Plains Road
Tarrytown, NY 10591

The text of this book is set in Veljovic Book 16/24
The illustrations are rendered in pen-and-ink and watercolor.
Printed in Hong Kong
1 2 3 4 5 6

Library of Congress Cataloging-in-Publication Data
Kiser, Kevin
Buzzy Widget / by Kevin Kiser ; illustrated by John O'Brien
p. cm.
Summary: Buzzy Widget builds robots to do his cooking and
cleaning but still finds there is something missing in his life.
ISBN 0-7614-5057-2
[1. Robots—Fiction 2. Conduct of Life—Fiction.] I. O'Brien,
John, date, ill. II. Title.
PZ7.K644Bu   1999   [E]—dc21   99-20041   CIP

Buzzy Widget liked to build things.

He built his car out of an old refrigerator from his junkyard.

He built his hair dryer from a broken-down windmil

He built his toaster from discarded rocket parts.

Buzzy Widget had built the perfect life for himself.

WIDGET'S
RECYCLATRON

Then one day, Buzzy woke up with the feeling that something was missing. He pulled out the list of everything he owned, and checked off each item, one by one. Nothing was missing—not so much as a paper clip.

Buzzy went to visit his neighbor Miss Jane.

"My life is no longer perfect," he told her. "Something is missing, but I don't know what."

"Maybe you are lonely, Buzzy," said Miss Jane. "Even geniuses sometimes need someone they can talk to."

"You could be right..." said Buzzy. Just then Buzzy's stomach growled. *Grrrooouuulp!* "Hey, I forgot to have breakfast! That must be it. I need someone to cook for me. I will build myself a CHEF!"

"Buzzy, you may be a genius, but even you can't *build* a chef!" said Miss Jane. But Buzzy was already halfway home.

Buzzy drilled and hammered and soldered and riveted all day and half the night. Finally he said, "My CHEF is ready!" He plugged it in and went to bed.

The next morning there was a wonderful smell in the air. It was bacon and eggs. And sausage. And oatmeal. And waffles. And orange juice. And hash browns. And every other breakfast food Buzzy liked.

"Hmmm," said Buzzy, "I think my CHEF needs a few adjustments."
Buzzy couldn't possibly eat everything, so he invited Miss
Jane over. She brought a jar of fresh clover honey, and they had
a very long, sweet breakfast.

A week later, the feeling of something missing came back, stronger than before.

Buzzy invited Miss Jane over to do a jigsaw puzzle.

"Your kitchen is a mess, Buzzy!" said Miss Jane.

"I'm afraid my CHEF doesn't do dishes," said Buzzy. "And I forget to do them myself."

"Maybe a CHEF is not exactly what you need..." said Miss Jane.

"You are absolutely right, Miss Jane!" Buzzy shouted. "My CHEF is not enough; I will build a MAID too!"

"That's not quite what I had in mind," said Miss Jane.

But Buzzy was already scribbling blueprints on his hand.

Buzzy drilled and hammered and soldered and riveted for two days and a night.

"At last," he said, "my MAID is ready!" He popped in four double-A batteries and went for a walk.

When Buzzy came home, his house was spotlessly clean—*too* clean!

"Not bad," said Buzzy, "it just needs a tweak or two..."

Then Buzzy took the MAID to show Miss Jane, and it cleaned her house too.

A few days later, while Buzzy was eating a scrumptious dinner in his perfectly clean house, the feeling of something missing came back again.

Buzzy took Miss Jane bowling.

"I have my CHEF and my MAID, but something is still missing," he told her.

"Buzzy, you can't build another robot every time you think something is missing in your life!" said Miss Jane. "What you need is someone to help you with EVERYTHING in your life, you need a partner ... a wife."

"A WIFE?" said Buzzy.

"Yes," said Miss Jane. "Husbands and wives always help each other with everything."

"You are exactly right, Miss Jane!" said Buzzy. "I do need a WIFE!"

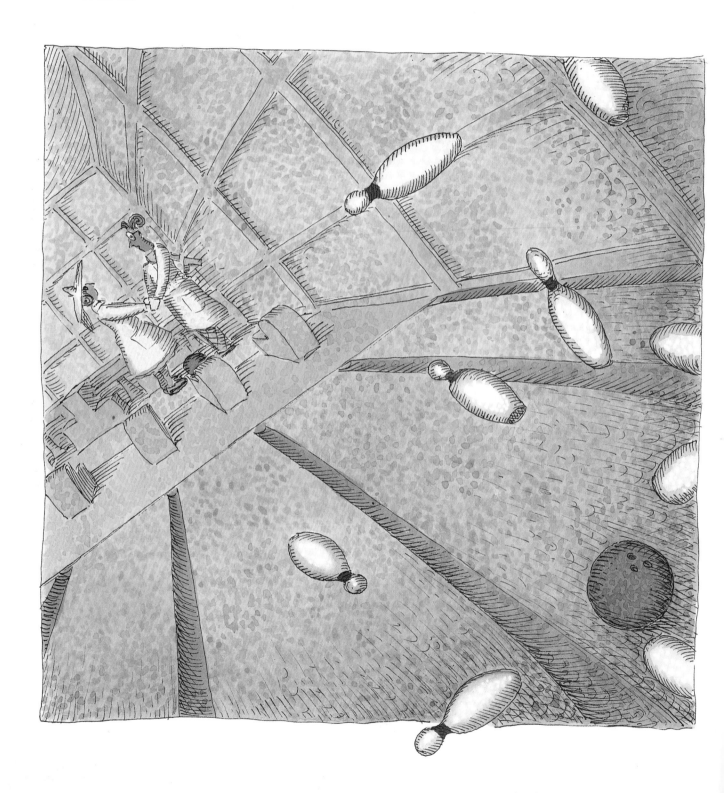

Buzzy kissed Miss Jane on the forehead and Miss Jane blushed.

"Well, I'd better go now," said Buzzy. "I must start building a WIFE, right away!"

"*Building* a wife?" said Miss Jane. "Buzzy Widget, you are the dumbest genius I have ever met!" But Buzzy was already headed out the door.

Buzzy drilled and hammered and soldered and riveted for one whole week and three minutes.

"That should do it," he said, yawning. "I never knew a WIFE would be so complicated!"

He switched it on and stepped back.

The WIFE began to work. It made Buzzy's bed. It washed his dishes.

It vacuumed and dusted and polished until the house was
spotlessly clean. Then it made dinner and plopped Buzzy down
at the table.

"Very efficient," said Buzzy.

Buzzy took a bite of his dinner. The WIFE snatched Buzzy's fork, washed it, and put it back in his hand. "Hmmm," said Buzzy.

When Buzzy went to his den, the WIFE followed behind him vacuuming where he had just walked. "Hmmm," said Buzzy.

Buzzy tried to do a jigsaw puzzle with the WIFE, but the WIFE kept putting the pieces back in the box. "Hmmm," said Buzzy.

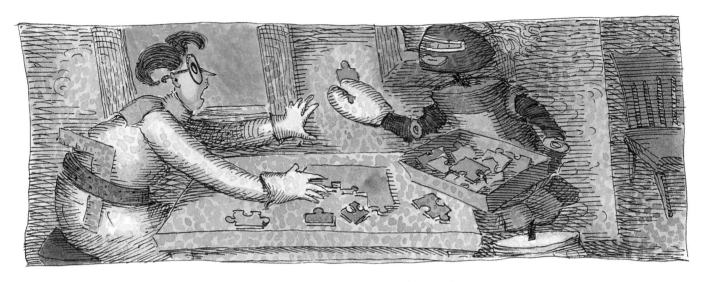

"Good night," said Buzzy when he went to bed. The WIFE didn't answer, it just remade the bed with him in it, tucking in the corners very tightly. "Hmmm," said Buzzy, "I guess efficiency isn't everything."

The next morning while Buzzy was rescuing his goldfish, there was a knock at the door.

"Hello, Buzzy," said Miss Jane. "Would you like to go on a picnic with me?"

"I would love to," said Buzzy, "but I don't know what my WIFE might do if I leave it alone right now."

"You still have a lot to learn about robots, Buzzy," said Miss Jane. She reached over and switched off the WIFE. "And even more to learn about wives."

"You are brilliant, Miss Jane!" said Buzzy. "If only you could help me find what's really missing from my life."

"Don't worry, Buzzy," said Miss Jane, taking his hand. "You're a genius—I'm sure you'll figure it out."

And with Miss Jane's help, he finally did...

...and Jane and Buzzy and their new pet lived perfectly ever after.